PIANO BLUES

Jessica jumped off the piano bench and dropped a curtsy. "Julie showed me how. Why don't you try it? We have to learn before the recital."

"I don't want to," Elizabeth said.

"It's easy," Jessica told her. "But we have to make sure we curtsy at the same time."

"I don't care!" Elizabeth yelled. "I don't want to curtsy! Curtsies are stupid and I hate them." CLLAANG! She hit the piano keys with her fist. "I hate this dumb piano too," she added. "I could be at the stables with Amy. It's all your fault I'm stuck here."

Elizabeth got up and ran upstairs.

"What's wrong with her?" Steven asked. "She sounds kind of angry."

Jessica smirked at him. "Mind your own business."

Bantam Books in the
SWEET VALLEY KIDS series

SWEET VALLEY KIDS

ELIZABETH'S PIANO LESSONS

Written by
Molly Mia Stewart

Created by
FRANCINE PASCAL

Illustrated by
Ying-Hwa Hu

BANTAM BOOKS
NEW YORK • TORONTO • LONDON • SYDNEY • AUCKLAND

RL 2, 005-008

ELIZABETH'S PIANO LESSONS
A Bantam Book / January 1994

*Sweet Valley High® and Sweet Valley Kids are
trademarks of Francine Pascal*

Conceived by Francine Pascal

*Produced by Daniel Weiss Associates, Inc.
33 West 17th Street
New York, NY 10011*

Cover art by Susan Tang

ISBN: 0-553-48102-9

Published simultaneously in the United States and Canada

*Bantam Books are published by Bantam Books, a division of Bantam
Doubleday Dell Publishing Group, Inc. Its trademark, consisting of the
words "Bantam Books" and the portrayal of a rooster, is Registered in
U.S. Patent and Trademark Office and in other countries. Marca
Registrada. Bantam Books, 1540 Broadway, New York, New York 10036.*

PRINTED IN THE UNITED STATES OF AMERICA

OPM   0 9 8 7 6 5 4 3 2

To Eli Garrett Stein

CHAPTER 1

Jessica's Secret

"Jessica, come on!" Elizabeth Wakefield yelled.

Elizabeth was standing in the Wakefields' driveway, waiting for her sister. If Jessica didn't hurry, the girls would both miss the school bus.

"What's taking you so long?" Elizabeth yelled. "Hurry up."

Elizabeth was always ready for school on time. Jessica never was. That was just one of the differences between the sisters.

Elizabeth liked to pretend she was a

space explorer or a scientist working at a jungle outpost. She was also a high scorer for her Sweet Valley Soccer League team. Elizabeth liked it when it rained the day before a game, because she loved playing on a muddy field. The muddier the field, the better she played.

Jessica didn't like soccer. She preferred less messy games such as hopscotch and jump rope. Jessica was one of the best jump-ropers at Sweet Valley Elementary School. And those games didn't get her clothes dirty. That was a big plus.

People were often surprised Elizabeth and Jessica had such different interests, because they looked exactly alike.

Jessica and Elizabeth were identical twins. Both girls had blue-green eyes and long blond hair with bangs. Sometimes they dressed in matching clothes just to confuse people. And even when

2

they didn't, their best friends in second grade often had to look twice before being sure which twin was which.

But no matter what they did, Elizabeth and Jessica almost *always* had fun together. Their differences didn't stop them from being best friends. They both thought it was extra, extra special to be twins.

"Here I am," Jessica said as she ran out and let the back door slam shut. "Let's go!"

They ran to the bus stop. The school bus was just pulling up.

Elizabeth and Jessica's brother, Steven, were waiting with other kids. He was only two years older than the twins, but he thought he was much more grown up.

"You almost missed the bus," Steven said.

"No problem," Jessica said. "You

would have held it for us. Right?"

"Held it?" Steven asked. "Why would I do that? I like to see you two pip-squeaks get in trouble. It's funny."

Jessica stuck her tongue out at him. She climbed up the steps of the bus in front of him and Elizabeth. Jessica chose a seat behind Julie Porter and Amy Sutton. Both girls were in the twins' class at school. Elizabeth slid into the seat next to Jessica.

"Hi," Amy greeted the twins. "I got to hear Julie play the piano last night." She had slept over at Julie's house. Other-wise Amy usually rode a different bus to school. "Julie is going to be great at the recital."

For days Julie had been telling her friends about her piano recital, which was coming up in a few weeks. A recital was a kind of musical performance. Julie was going to play "Farmer in the Dell" all by herself on a stage at the Sweet Valley Public Library. All of the kids who took lessons with Julie's piano teacher would be performing.

"I'm a little nervous," Julie said. "A lot of people are coming."

"Have you decided what to wear yet?" Jessica asked.

"My mom bought me a new dress yesterday," Julie said. "It's peach-colored with a big white ribbon in back."

"That sounds pretty," Jessica said. "I wish I could get a fancy new dress."

"I even got new black shoes," Julie added. "My mom thinks it's a big day. She says she's going to take lots of pictures and have the best one blown up and framed."

"Playing in a recital must be neat," Jessica said. She loved being the center of attention. "I wish I was going to be in it."

"You could come hear me play," Julie said. "But you can't be in the recital unless you take piano lessons."

Jessica smiled. "Well, maybe we're going to *start* taking lessons."

"What do you mean?" Elizabeth asked.

Jessica just smiled some more. "Wait and see."

Elizabeth had a funny feeling. She felt as if Jessica knew something she didn't. But before Elizabeth could find out what that was, Amy changed the subject.

"I'm starting horseback-riding lessons," Amy announced. "My first one is today after school."

When Elizabeth heard that, she forgot all about Jessica's mysterious behavior. "That's great! Did I tell you I took riding lessons over Thanksgiving vacation?"

"When you were on the Indian reservation?" Julie asked.

"Right," Elizabeth said. "It was the best."

"Do you want to take lessons with me?" Amy asked, looking first at Elizabeth, then at Jessica. "That would make it even more fun."

"I'd love to!" Elizabeth said.

"You could come with me today and sign up," Amy suggested.

Jessica shook her head. "No way. I'm not getting near another stable. They stink."

Amy laughed, but Elizabeth frowned.

"I like stables," Elizabeth told Jessica. "And I don't think they stink."

Jessica shrugged. "I'd rather take piano lessons, like Julie."

"Riding lessons are much better than piano lessons," Elizabeth said. "You'd

never catch me stuck on a piano bench."

Amy and Julie exchanged looks. Jessica and Elizabeth almost never fought. But they both sounded angry now.

"That's what you think," Jessica said.

"What do you mean?" Elizabeth asked.

Jessica didn't answer Elizabeth. She stared out the window with a sly smile.

CHAPTER 2

Trapped

"Hi, I'm home!" Elizabeth yelled as she let herself in the front door that afternoon.

Upstairs, Jessica jumped off her bed. Elizabeth had gone to the stables with Amy after school. Jessica had come home alone. She felt as if she had been waiting forever for Elizabeth to get back. Jessica ran downstairs as fast as she could. She wanted to talk to Elizabeth before their mother did.

"Hi, Liz," Jessica said, walking into the kitchen.

"Hi, Jess!" Elizabeth picked an apple out of the fruit bowl on the table and took a small bite. "You should have come to the stables with me and Amy," she said as she chewed. "We had the greatest time. First we—"

"Forget about that," Jessica said. "I have something important to tell you."

"What?" Elizabeth asked.

"Aunt Helen called," Jessica said.

Aunt Helen was actually Jessica and Elizabeth's great-aunt. She was one of the twins' favorite relatives.

"Really?" Elizabeth asked. "What did she say?"

"She wants to pay for you and me and Steven to take any kind of lessons we want," Jessica announced.

Elizabeth's eyes widened. "Really? Terrific. Boy, are we going to be busy. We already have modern-dance class.

And I have soccer. Now we both get to do something else."

"Steven wants to go to basketball camp next summer," Jessica said. "Hurray! A whole week without him."

"Not bad," Elizabeth agreed. "When did Aunt Helen call?"

"Huh . . . before school," Jessica said. "You were already outside. That's why I was late. And I kind of—kind of told her we wanted piano lessons."

Elizabeth's mouth dropped open. "You did? Why?"

"Because that's what I want," Jessica said.

"Well, you may want piano lessons, but I don't," Elizabeth said, putting her unfinished apple down on the table. "Anyway, you only want to learn the piano because Julie's going to be in that recital."

"So what?" Jessica asked.

"So a few weeks ago you didn't care about the piano at all," Elizabeth said. "You didn't even listen to Julie talk—"

She didn't finish her sentence because Mrs. Wakefield came into the kitchen. "I'm glad you're home, Elizabeth," Mrs. Wakefield said. "I guess Jessica told you about Aunt Helen's generous offer. She's thrilled you two want to take piano lessons. Aunt Helen loves music."

Elizabeth frowned and glared at Jessica.

Jessica looked away. She knew Elizabeth wanted to take riding lessons. But she also knew Elizabeth wouldn't want to disappoint Aunt Helen. Jessica wasn't sure what Elizabeth would do.

"Are you excited about the big news, Elizabeth?" Mrs. Wakefield asked. "You were outside when Aunt Helen called this morning. But Jessica told me you've both been wanting piano lessons for a long time."

Jessica crossed her fingers for luck. She knew she hadn't been one hundred percent honest with her mother. But she was almost positive Elizabeth wouldn't tell on her.

"Sounds fine," Elizabeth said after a long pause.

"Good." Mrs. Wakefield smiled. "How were the stables?"

"They were great," Elizabeth said. "Amy almost fell off her horse, though. She got a little mad because I started to laugh."

Mrs. Wakefield shook her head. "I'm glad you two didn't choose riding lessons. The piano is much safer."

"Yeah," Elizabeth said. "Nothing much can happen to you sitting on a dumb bench."

Mrs. Wakefield gave Elizabeth a puzzled look. But before she could say anything, Jessica grabbed Elizabeth's hand. "Come upstairs, Liz," Jessica said. "I started to build a house of cards."

As soon as they got to their room, Jessica gave Elizabeth a hug. "Thanks! I know you'll like piano lessons once we start."

Elizabeth shook her head. "Why didn't you tell me sooner that Aunt Helen called?"

"I was going to," Jessica said. "But this morning on the bus, I decided to make it a surprise."

"You tricked me," Elizabeth said. She sounded angry.

Jessica shrugged. "Piano lessons will be fun. Besides, it's too late for you to back out now. Aunt Helen might get upset."

CHAPTER 3

Too Late

The next day Elizabeth woke up in a bad mood. It was Saturday, so she and Jessica didn't have to hurry to school. They had all day to play. But Elizabeth still felt crabby. She was mad Jessica had tricked her.

Elizabeth jumped out of bed. She had decided to tell her parents she didn't want to take piano lessons. Elizabeth planned to say she had changed her mind. That way Jessica wouldn't get into trouble for lying.

Elizabeth got dressed without making

a sound. She didn't want to wake Jessica up. She didn't want Jessica to have a chance to try to change her mind.

When Elizabeth got to the kitchen, Mr. Wakefield was drinking coffee and reading the paper. Steven was eating a huge stack of blueberry pancakes. Mrs. Wakefield was hanging up the phone.

"Good morning, sweetie," Mr. Wakefield said, looking up.

"Good morning," Elizabeth answered.

"Hmmrmm," Steven said. His mouth was full.

"I just finished talking to Julie's mother," Mrs. Wakefield told Elizabeth. "She gave me the name of Julie's piano teacher. Mrs. Porter says Julie likes him a lot."

"Uh, I—" Elizabeth started to say.

"Did you know Julie's mother teaches music at Sweet Valley High and that her father is a conductor?" Mrs. Wakefield cut her off. "They sure are a musical family."

"I know, but—" Elizabeth tried again.

"Mrs. Porter told me her husband began taking violin lessons when he was just about your age," Mrs. Wakefield interrupted again.

"I—"

This time Mr. Wakefield kept Elizabeth from finishing her sentence. "Maybe you'll be a musician when you grow up, too."

"Maybe," Elizabeth mumbled. She pulled out a chair and sat down at the table.

"I'm sorry, honey, did you want to say something?" Mrs. Wakefield asked. "I'm so excited for you that I got carried away."

Elizabeth gulped. She took a deep

breath and then . . . chickened out. "Please pass the pancakes and syrup," she said.

Jessica came into the kitchen. "Good morning, everybody."

"Good morning, Jessica," Mrs. Wakefield said. "I was just telling Elizabeth I found you a piano teacher."

"Is it Julie's?" Jessica asked. Mrs. Wakefield nodded and Jessica yelled, "Yippee."

"What do you say we go to the music store and look at pianos after breakfast?" Mr. Wakefield suggested. "You'll need one to practice on."

Jessica looked at Elizabeth with a big smile on her face. "All right! That way we can start taking lessons right away."

Elizabeth swallowed a bite of her pancakes, but they didn't taste good today. Nothing could taste good when she was about to start lessons she didn't want. *There's no way I can tell them now,* she told herself. *It's too late.*

A little while later the Wakefields drove to downtown Sweet Valley and parked in front of a music store. There were many kinds of different instruments in the window. As they went inside, Steven wandered off to bang on a drum set. Elizabeth and Jessica and their parents headed toward a group of pianos.

"Look at that one," Jessica said, pointing. "It's so big!"

Elizabeth was still upset with Jessica. But she had to admit the piano Jessica was pointing to was beautiful. Its wooden case shone. The top was propped open so you could see the strings inside.

A salesman came up to them. "May I help you folks?"

"We'd like to rent a piano," Mrs. Wakefield said.

Jessica pulled on her mother's sleeve. "How about that one?" She pointed again to the big, beautiful piano.

"That's called a grand piano," the salesman told Jessica. He smiled at Mr. and Mrs. Wakefield. "Would you like to look at it?"

Mrs. Wakefield laughed. "A grand piano wouldn't fit in our living room unless we got rid of the couch. How about something smaller?"

"Fine," the salesman agreed. "Let me show you some uprights."

The salesman led the Wakefields to a bunch of smaller pianos. The uprights had flat backs and could easily be placed against a wall. Elizabeth and Jessica agreed they were pretty, too.

"This one looks like the one at school," Elizabeth said, running her hand over a white piano. Once in a while Mrs. Otis, the twins' teacher, played a song on the piano in the school music room. Mr. and Mrs. Wakefield picked out a wooden upright and signed some papers. Then the Wakefields went home and waited. A few hours later a big truck pulled up in front of their house.

Elizabeth and Jessica ran outside to watch. Two men with big muscles pulled the piano out of the truck and then picked it up. The piano must have been heavy, because the men made awful faces as they carried it into the house and set it down in the living room.

"Let's try it," Jessica said as soon as the men had gone. She sat on the piano bench that had also been delivered and hit a few keys.

"Move over a little," Elizabeth said. "I want to try it, too." She pushed down keys with all ten of her fingers.

Steven put his hands over his ears. "Get them some lessons fast!"

"I think it sounds wonderful," Mrs. Wakefield said. "And soon you'll be making beautiful music."

Elizabeth smiled. She'd been trying to cheer up. She still didn't want to take piano lessons. But she also didn't want to disappoint her parents or Aunt Helen. Besides, Jessica seemed really happy. Maybe taking piano lessons wouldn't be so bad.

CHAPTER 4

Jessica's First Lesson

"Tell me about your piano lessons," Caroline Pearce said to Elizabeth and Jessica after school on Tuesday.

Caroline was sitting in the bus seat behind the twins. Jessica and Elizabeth hadn't told Caroline about their lessons, but somehow she always knew everything everyone in Mrs. Otis's class was up to. Jessica thought Caroline was a busybody, but she was excited about her piano lessons. She didn't mind talking about them.

"My first lesson is at three thirty

today and Elizabeth's is at four," Jessica said proudly. "Our teacher's name is Leo Wheeler. Julie takes lessons from him, too." She looked around for Julie and finally spotted her near the front of the bus. It was too far to shout and include Julie in the conversation.

Elizabeth didn't say anything. She looked grumpy.

"Leo's house is real close to the park," Jessica went on. "We can walk there. Elizabeth can wait while I have my lesson. Then I'll wait for her."

"No way," Elizabeth spoke up. "I'm staying at the park until right before my lesson. I'm not going to Leo's until the very last second."

"OK, OK," Jessica said. "Do whatever you want." She didn't understand why Elizabeth was being so weird about taking piano lessons. Still, Jessica wasn't worried. She was positive Elizabeth would be happy about the lessons once they started.

After they ate their snack, Jessica walked with Elizabeth as far as the park. Then Jessica walked toward Leo's house by herself. She climbed the steps to Leo's porch and rang the doorbell.

A tall man with a beard answered the door. "Hello there, I'm Leo Wheeler."

Jessica smiled. "My name is Jessica Wakefield. I'm here for my first lesson. My sister, Elizabeth, is coming later."

Leo showed Jessica inside. Mrs. Wheeler came out to say hello. She held a crying baby in her arms and quickly disappeared into another room. Leo led Jessica into the living room and told her to sit on a bench in front of a grand piano even bigger than the one in the store.

Leo taught Jessica the names of the

keys. Then he played a scale for her. His fingers were long and skinny. He made playing the scale look easy.

"OK, your turn now," Leo said. "Try it with just your right hand first."

Jessica put her right hand on the keys. She put her thumb on middle C just as Leo had showed her. Jessica tried to play the scale. The first three notes were easy. But then came a tricky part where you had to cross your thumb underneath your other fingers. Jessica's hand was small. She had to stretch her thumb to reach the fourth key. Still, she did her best.

"Great job," Leo said. "You have talent!"

Jessica grinned. She loved compliments. She liked Leo.

Next, Leo showed Jessica how to play the scale with her left hand. He was

patient when she made mistakes. By the time the lesson was half-over, Jessica could play the scale with both hands together.

"I'm planning a recital for the Sunday after next," Leo told Jessica when they had finished. "All of my students are going to perform."

"I know," Jessica said. "Julie Porter is in my class at school. She told me and Elizabeth all about the recital."

"Would you like to be in it?" Leo asked. "You and your sister could perform a duet. That means you would play different parts of the same song at the same time. Since you would be playing together, you would have more fun practicing."

"Wow!" Jessica said. She wanted to jump up with happiness. "That sounds great."

"It's going to take a lot of work to learn a song in just two weeks," Leo warned her. "You'll have to practice doubly hard."

"I—we—don't mind," Jessica said. "The recital sounds neat!"

Leo nodded. "Let's run through the song I'd like you to play a few times together. Since you haven't learned to read music yet, I'll write down the names of the keys for you."

Jessica could hardly believe her luck. She and Elizabeth were going to be in the recital! Jessica couldn't wait for the big day. She already pictured herself on stage. And she imagined the audience standing up to applaud—and shouting for them to play a second song.

CHAPTER 5

Trapped Again

Elizabeth kicked the soccer ball to Todd Wilkins. "Here, take this. I have to go now."

Todd stopped the ball with his foot. "You can't leave. We're already behind by two goals. We need you."

Elizabeth and her friends were playing soccer on a grassy field at the park. Elizabeth had scored her team's only goal and she was having a lot of fun, but her watch said three fifty-six. That meant her piano lesson started in just four minutes.

"I don't want to go," Elizabeth said. "I *have* to. Now."

"Why?" Todd insisted. "It's early."

Elizabeth still hadn't told all her friends about her new lessons.

"I have a—a piano lesson," Elizabeth muttered.

"You do?" Todd's mouth dropped open. "How come?"

Elizabeth groaned. "I don't have time to tell you in four minutes."

Kisho Murasaki was playing goalie. "Hey, Elizabeth!" he called to her as she started to leave. "Where are you going?"

Elizabeth pretended not to hear Kisho's question. " 'Bye, everybody," she yelled. "See you tomorrow at school."

Elizabeth ran the few blocks to Leo's. As she got near Leo's house, she saw Jessica come out the door and run toward her down the sidewalk.

"Guess what, guess what," Jessica shouted. She stopped in front of Elizabeth. "We're going to be in the recital! See? I told you it was a good idea to learn the piano."

"How can we be in the recital?" Elizabeth asked. "We don't know how to play anything."

"Leo's giving us an easy song to learn," Jessica explained. "And we're going to practice lots and lots."

"I don't want to be in the recital," Elizabeth said.

"Why not?" Jessica asked. "It's the best part."

"Because I don't want to," Elizabeth said, crossing her arms stubbornly.

"You have to," Jessica insisted. "Leo wants us to play a song together, and I said we would."

Elizabeth stomped her foot. "You should

have asked me first! And you should have asked me before you told everyone I wanted to take piano lessons."

Jessica shrugged. "I already said I was sorry. Now, you'll play in the recital, right?"

"Only if I can't think of a way out of it," Elizabeth said.

"You won't," Jessica said. "I'm going home to practice. Leo is waiting for you. 'Bye!"

Jessica took off toward their house.

Elizabeth walked quickly the rest of the way. She was madder than ever. Jessica was being worse than bossy. She was acting as if Elizabeth couldn't make decisions for herself.

Elizabeth held her finger to the Wheelers' doorbell for a long time.

The door finally opened. "Hi. I'm Leo. You must be Elizabeth Wakefield."

"I guess so," Elizabeth said.

"You're a little late," Leo said. "Try to be on time from now on. A half hour isn't much time. We'll need to use all of it."

Elizabeth felt her face grow hot. "Sorry," she told Leo. "I'm not usually late."

"No problem," Leo said. He introduced Elizabeth to Mrs. Wheeler when she popped her head out. Then Leo showed Elizabeth to the piano. Elizabeth thought it was beautiful, but she was too angry to say so. She plopped down on the bench.

"Why don't you start by hitting some notes?" Leo suggested.

Elizabeth stared at the keys. She thought about the recital. She thought of spending hours and hours practicing. She thought of Todd and Kisho playing soccer without her.

With all her might Elizabeth crashed

all ten fingers into the keys. The piano made a huge, ugly sound. Elizabeth smiled. Maybe Leo would tell her she didn't have talent. Maybe he would tell her never to come back.

But Leo smiled, too. "That was good and loud. Now let's work on making it sound a little nicer."

CHAPTER 6

Practice Makes Perfect

"Liz, pay attention," Jessica said four days later.

Elizabeth wiggled on the piano bench. "I *am* paying attention," she said. But they both knew that wasn't true.

Jessica and Elizabeth were practicing their duet, "Mary Had a Little Lamb." It wasn't much harder to play than a scale. They knew just how it should sound, because they'd learned the words years ago. The song started like this:

Mary had a little lamb,

little lamb, little lamb.
Mary had a little lamb,
whose fleece was white as snow.

Jessica could already play the song by heart. She was concentrating hard on practicing. Elizabeth was daydreaming. She made lots of mistakes.

As they played, they sang along under their breath. So far, they hadn't gotten to the first "lamb" without Elizabeth's making a mistake.

Together they sang, "Mary had a lit—"

Bllinng.

Elizabeth dropped her hands off the keys. "Guess what Eva told me today?" Eva Simpson was one of their friends from school.

Jessica sighed. "What?"

"She promised to teach me how to swim backstroke," Elizabeth said.

"That's nice, I guess," Jessica said. "Let's start at the beginning."

Elizabeth groaned. "Do we have to? The recital isn't for over a week. We've got plenty of time to learn our song."

"The recital isn't for a while," Jessica agreed. "But our next lesson is in just a few days. I want Leo to see how hard we're working. I want him to say we're getting good fast."

Elizabeth sighed. "OK, let's try it again."

They started over, singing, "Mary had a little—"

Bllanng.

"Pay attention!" Jessica ordered.

"I *am* paying attention," Elizabeth insisted.

"Then pay double attention," Jessica said.

She was beginning to worry about Elizabeth. After all, they were supposed to play a *duet* at the recital. Jessica wanted to do a great job. She practiced for at least an hour every day. But Elizabeth never practiced for more than a few minutes. Suddenly, Jessica hoped her sister wouldn't embarrass her in front of everyone.

"Mary had—"

Bllonng.

Steven came out of the den. "I thought you guys were supposed to be twins."

"We are twins," Elizabeth told him.

"Not on the piano, you're not," Steven said. "Jessica is much better."

Jessica smiled. "Come on, Liz. Try it again."

"Mary had a little—"

Bllinng.

Jessica shook her head. "Maybe a break will help. Did Julie tell you she's going to curtsy after she plays?"

"No," Elizabeth said, sulking.

"She showed me how." Jessica jumped up off the piano bench and dropped a curtsy. "Why don't you try it? We have to learn before the recital."

"I don't want to," Elizabeth said.

"It's easy," Jessica told her. "But we have to make sure we curtsy at the same time."

"I don't care!" Elizabeth yelled. "I don't want to curtsy! Curtsies are stupid and I hate them." CLLAANG! She hit the piano keys with her fist. "I hate this dumb piano, too," she added. "I could be at the stables with Amy. It's all your fault I'm stuck here."

Elizabeth got up and ran upstairs.

"What's wrong with her?" Steven asked. "She sounds kind of angry."

Jessica smirked at him. "Mind your own business."

43

Suddenly Jessica was in a bad mood, but she sat back down at the piano and played the song all the way through without making a mistake. "There," she said. "Elizabeth could learn the song perfectly if she just wanted to."

But Jessica knew the problem was Elizabeth *didn't* want to. That made Jessica mad. She thought Elizabeth was being a big baby about piano lessons.

CHAPTER 7

Venus

The following Tuesday, it rained. Mrs. Otis's class had to spend morning recess inside. Elizabeth and Amy helped each other put a puzzle together.

"There's a new horse at the stables," Amy told Elizabeth. "I rode her during my last lesson. Her name is Venus. And know what? I think she likes me."

Elizabeth fitted in a corner piece. "I know what you mean. The horse I rode at the reservation was always rubbing me with her nose. It was like a horse hug."

"Venus does that, too!" Amy said.

Elizabeth sighed. "I wish I could meet her."

"You can," Amy said. "Come with me to the stables this afternoon. I have a lesson."

"OK," Elizabeth agreed. "Thanks."

That afternoon Elizabeth rushed out of class as soon as the bell rang. She and Amy ran outside, where Mrs. Sutton was waiting to drive Amy to the stables. Elizabeth climbed into the Suttons' car. She was excited. All she could think about was meeting Venus.

When Elizabeth got home a few hours later, she felt terrific. She'd had a great time at the stables.

"Is that you, Liz?" Mrs. Wakefield called out as Elizabeth walked in the door.

"Yes," Elizabeth answered.

"Please come in here," Mrs. Wakefield said sternly. "I'd like to talk to you."

Elizabeth felt worried. Her mother sounded angry. She walked into the den. Jessica and Mrs. Wakefield were sitting together on the couch. Mrs. Wakefield was holding one of the twins' favorite books.

"I was worried about you this afternoon," Mrs. Wakefield told Elizabeth. "I didn't know where you were."

Elizabeth swallowed hard. She knew what was wrong now. She hadn't asked permission before going to the stables.

"Jessica didn't know where you were, either," Mrs. Wakefield went on. "She and Steven both missed the bus home waiting for you. We were all concerned. So was Mrs. Otis."

"I went to the stables with Amy," Elizabeth whispered.

"I know," Mrs. Wakefield said. "I spoke to Amy's mother."

"I'm sorry, Mom," Elizabeth said.

Mrs. Wakefield sighed. "You know the rules, Elizabeth. You have to talk to me or your dad before going somewhere with a friend. Last time you called me from school to ask permission. You should have done that. I don't want this to happen again."

"It won't," Elizabeth promised.

"You missed your piano lesson, too," Jessica said with a big frown on her face.

Elizabeth gasped. "Oh, no! I forgot."

"If we're going to be good at the recital, we have to practice," Jessica said. "We have to practice every day. And we can't miss lessons. I don't want to be up on stage and have everyone laugh at us."

"I'm sorry," Elizabeth repeated, hanging her head.

"It's not like you to just disappear," Mrs. Wakefield said. She looked thoughtful. "Don't you like taking piano lessons?"

"Yes," Elizabeth lied. She couldn't tell her mother the truth. She already felt awful for worrying her. And she didn't want to disappoint her even more.

But Elizabeth felt only a tiny bit bad Jessica was mad at her. After all, Jessica had gotten her into this mess. Elizabeth was mad at her, too.

CHAPTER 8

A Visitor

On the day before the recital, the Wakefields' doorbell rang while Jessica and Elizabeth were practicing. Mrs. Wakefield wasn't at home. Steven and Mr. Wakefield were watching a basketball game on television.

"Girls!" Mr. Wakefield called from the den. "Could one of you please get that? Someone's about to make an important shot."

"OK, Dad." Jessica jumped up from the piano bench. "Keep practicing," she ordered Elizabeth as she ran to the front door. She threw it open. Mrs. Wakefield was standing on the stoop.

"Hi, Mom," Jessica said, feeling confused. "Why are you ringing the bell?"

Mrs. Wakefield took a big step sideways. She had been hiding someone behind her.

"Surprise!" that someone yelled.

"Aunt Helen!" Jessica shouted.

Elizabeth spun around on the piano bench. When she saw who was at the door, she jumped up and ran to give her aunt a kiss.

Mr. Wakefield and Steven came out of the den. They each gave Aunt Helen a hug.

"What are you doing here?" Steven asked her.

"Staying with us for the weekend," Mrs. Wakefield said.

"You can come to the recital tomorrow," Jessica said, bouncing up and down.

"That was the idea," Mrs. Wakefield told her.

Elizabeth and Jessica exchanged happy looks. They loved Aunt Helen. They were glad she had come to visit.

"Do you want to hear our recital song?" Jessica asked her.

"I have to clean the pool," Mr. Wakefield said quickly.

"I'll help you," Mrs. Wakefield said. She followed him out of the room.

Steven started to laugh. "Mom and Dad sure are busy all of a sudden. Wonder if your piano playing has something to do with it."

"Very funny," Jessica said. "Aunt Helen, do you want to hear our song?" she asked again.

"That sounds wonderful," Aunt Helen said.

"Jessica," Elizabeth said, "Aunt Helen just got here."

"So?" Jessica asked.

"So maybe she's hungry," Elizabeth said.

Aunt Helen shook her head.

"Do you want something to drink?" Elizabeth asked her.

Aunt Helen shook her head again.

"Do you need to take a nap?" Elizabeth asked.

Aunt Helen laughed. "I'm fine, Elizabeth. But thanks for your concern."

"Come on, Liz," Jessica said. "Let's play."

"OK," Elizabeth said. "But first I have to take Aunt Helen's suitcase to her room."

"I'll do it," Steven offered. He grabbed the bag and started up the stairs.

Elizabeth gave Steven a dirty look.

"Come on, Elizabeth," Jessica insisted. She went to sit in front of the piano.

"Guess what," Elizabeth said to Aunt Helen.

"What?" Aunt Helen said.

"I got a new book," Elizabeth told her. "You can read it if you want. It's a really neat mystery. First a big—"

"E-liz-a-beth," Jessica interrupted. "I'm waiting. So is Aunt Helen."

Elizabeth shuffled over to the piano bench and sat down.

"Play it straight through," Jessica whispered. "Even if you make a mistake."

They played their song. Elizabeth made tons of mistakes.

"That was wonderful," Aunt Helen said. "I can't believe how much you two have learned in just a few weeks."

"I thought it was terrible!" Steven said, coming back down the stairs.

Jessica frowned. "We need more practice. Especially Elizabeth. We'll do better next time."

They played their song again. Elizabeth made mistake after mistake again. They ran through the song another time. Elizabeth made even *more* mistakes. And the more mistakes Elizabeth made, the angrier she got.

"You're not trying, Liz," Jessica said. "I know you could play it right if you just concentrated."

They started over. They weren't singing out loud, but Jessica could hear the words in her head.

"Mary had a little lamb, little—"

Bllinng.

Steven put his hands over his ears and ran out of the room. Jessica cringed, but she kept playing. "—lamb, little lamb. Mary had a—"

Bllanng.

Aunt Helen started to clap right in the middle of the song. "That was much better! I think you girls have earned a break. Who wants to go for a walk?"

"I do!" Elizabeth said. She jumped off the piano bench.

"No, thanks," Jessica said. "I'm going to stay here. The recital is *tomorrow,* Elizabeth."

"I know," Elizabeth said, opening the door. "See you later."

After Elizabeth and Aunt Helen had gone, Jessica pounded the keys in anger. She was beginning to think it had been a bad idea to trick Elizabeth into taking piano lessons. Jessica knew *she* wouldn't mess up at the recital. She knew the song perfectly. But Elizabeth was going to be terrible—mundo terrible. If only Elizabeth didn't have to play.

CHAPTER 9

Rescued

"Is your piano teacher nice?" Aunt Helen asked Elizabeth.

The two of them were walking down the Wakefields' shady street.

"Uh, yes," Elizabeth said. "But I always have to do everything over and over." She pulled Aunt Helen's hand. "Want to see the park where Jessica and I play? It's not a long walk."

"OK," Aunt Helen agreed. "What's your piano teacher's name?"

"Leo," Elizabeth said. She pointed to Caroline's house as they walked by.

"A girl in my class lives there."

"What a pretty house," Aunt Helen said. "So, your piano lessons are fun?"

"Well, they're . . . they're OK," Elizabeth said. "Guess what?"

Aunt Helen smiled. "What?"

"My friend Amy is taking horseback-riding lessons," Elizabeth said. "She rides a beautiful horse named Venus. She's exactly the same color as a penny, except for her feet. They're white. I wish *I* could ride Venus."

"Really?" Aunt Helen asked. "Have you ever ridden a horse before?"

"I rode one for the first time on our trip to the Mohave reservation," Elizabeth told her. "Did you know we went there?"

Aunt Helen nodded.

"That was so neat," Elizabeth said. "The best part was the horses. I took a bunch of riding lessons—every day. Do you like to ride horses, Aunt Helen?"

"Well, I haven't been on one for a long, long time," Aunt Helen answered. "But I remember how much fun it was."

Elizabeth sighed. "It's great."

Aunt Helen nodded, looking thoughtful. "Did I ever tell you I took piano lessons when I was about your age?"

Elizabeth shook her head.

"I took lessons for four years," Aunt Helen said.

Elizabeth studied the cracks in the sidewalk. "I bet you loved them."

Aunt Helen shook her head. "I hated them."

"Really?" Elizabeth was so surprised, she stopped walking.

"I couldn't stand the piano," Aunt Helen said. "But I kept on taking lessons for all those years. You know why?"

"No," Elizabeth said. "Why?"

"I was afraid to tell my mother the truth," Aunt Helen said. "I thought she'd be disappointed. But do you know what happened when I finally told her?"

"What?" Elizabeth asked.

Aunt Helen sighed. "She didn't mind my quitting at all. She said she thought the lessons made *me* happy. I wish I had told her the truth years earlier. I could have saved myself a lot of grief."

Elizabeth and Aunt Helen started to walk again.

"Is there something you'd like to tell me?" Aunt Helen asked gently.

"Jessica was the one who wanted piano lessons," Elizabeth blurted out. "Leo's really nice, but I don't like playing the piano. And I hate practicing! I miss being outside with my friends."

Aunt Helen took Elizabeth's hand. "I

63

understand," she said. "And I'm glad you told me."

Elizabeth grinned. It felt good to get the truth out.

"Tell me more about the stables," Aunt Helen said. "Are they far away? Does your friend like her instructor?"

CHAPTER 10

Elizabeth's Surprise

Jessica hit the final note. She smiled. She hadn't made any mistakes.

With a big grin Jessica stood up and faced the audience. Everyone was applauding her. She could see her parents, Aunt Helen, Steven—and Elizabeth in the second row. Elizabeth was smiling. Even Steven was clapping.

Jessica curtsied.

"Hurray," Elizabeth yelled.

After the recital was over, all of the students and their guests had cookies and punch.

"Your song was pretty," Elizabeth told Julie.

"Thanks," Julie said. "How come you didn't play?"

Elizabeth smiled. "My parents aren't making me take piano lessons anymore. I'm really happy."

"Hi, Liz." Elizabeth spun around. Leo was standing behind her.

Elizabeth gulped. "Oh—hi."

"I just wanted you to know you shouldn't feel bad about quitting," Leo said. "If you didn't like the piano, it was the right thing to do."

Elizabeth smiled. "Thanks."

When everyone was ready to go, Mr. Wakefield suggested they take a drive. In the car Elizabeth was busy talking to Jessica and Aunt Helen. She didn't notice where they were going.

Elizabeth was surprised when her father

turned the station wagon in at the stables. "What are we doing here?" she asked.

"Signing you up for riding lessons," Aunt Helen announced.

For a moment Elizabeth was too surprised to say anything. Then she gave Aunt Helen a big hug. "Thanks," she whispered. "You're the best."

"No problem," Aunt Helen said.

Elizabeth jumped out of the car. "I'll give you a tour. And you can meet Venus."

Everyone started toward the stables.

"Aren't you afraid Elizabeth will fall off her horse?" Jessica asked Mrs. Wakefield as they walked. "I thought you were glad we didn't want to take riding lessons."

Elizabeth's eyes widened. "Jess," she hissed.

Jessica covered her mouth with her hand. "Sorry, Liz."

Elizabeth was worried. Her mother might decide riding lessons were too dangerous.

But Mrs. Wakefield just smiled. "I know Liz will be extra careful."

"I will," Elizabeth promised.

Mr. and Mrs. Wakefield signed Elizabeth up for lessons. She was going to come to the stables on the same day as Amy. Elizabeth was so excited, she could hardly stand still.

"Are you mad at me?" Jessica asked Elizabeth in the car on the way home.

"I'm not mad," Elizabeth said. "But from now on you've got to ask me before you say I'll do something."

"I'm sorry," Jessica said. "Sometimes I forget we don't have to do everything together."

"Especially not take piano lessons," Elizabeth said.

Jessica laughed. "You mean especially not take *riding* lessons."

The next day at school, Mrs. Otis led the class to the music room in the afternoon.

"We have a special treat. As some of you know, Julie and Jessica were in a piano recital over the weekend," the teacher said as everyone crowded into the room. "I asked them if they would like to play their songs for the class, and they both said yes."

Jessica smiled at Elizabeth. She knew her sister had been the one to tell Mrs. Otis all about the recital first thing when they got to school.

"Julie, why don't you go first?" Mrs. Otis said.

Jessica wiped her palms on her jeans as Julie played. She was excited and a little nervous all over again. Then it was her turn. She played "Mary Had a Little Lamb." Everyone in the class applauded when she finished.

Mrs. Otis clapped the loudest. "That was beautiful!"

"Nice job," Elizabeth told Jessica after she sat down.

"Thanks for telling Mrs. Otis," Jessica said. "You're the nicest sister in the world."

"And Mrs. Otis is the nicest teacher in the world," Elizabeth added.

Jessica nodded. "I wish she could be our teacher forever."

"Well, she can't be our teacher *forever*," Elizabeth said. "But she will be our teacher for the rest of second grade."

Is Elizabeth right? Or could the twins get a new teacher—sooner than they think? Find out in Sweet Valley Kids #46, GET THE TEACHER!

SIGN UP FOR THE SWEET VALLEY HIGH® FAN CLUB!

Hey, girls! Get all the gossip on Sweet Valley High's® most popular teenagers when you join our fantastic Fan Club! As a member, you'll get all of this really cool stuff:

- Membership Card with your own personal Fan Club ID number
- A Sweet Valley High® Secret Treasure Box
- Sweet Valley High® Stationery
- Official Fan Club Pencil (for secret note writing!)
- Three Bookmarks
- A "Members Only" Door Hanger
- Two Skeins of J. & P. Coats® Embroidery Floss with flower barrette instruction leaflet
- Two editions of *The Oracle* newsletter
- Plus exclusive Sweet Valley High® product offers, special savings, contests, and much more!

Be the first to find out what Jessica & Elizabeth Wakefield are up to by joining the Sweet Valley High® Fan Club for the one-year membership fee of only $6.25 each for U.S. residents, $8.25 for Canadian residents (U.S. currency). Includes shipping & handling.

Send a check or money order (do not send cash) made payable to "Sweet Valley High® Fan Club" along with this form to:

SWEET VALLEY HIGH® FAN CLUB, BOX 3919-B, SCHAUMBURG, IL 60168-3919

NAME_____
(Please print clearly)

ADDRESS_____

CITY_____ STATE _____ ZIP_____
(Required)

AGE _____ BIRTHDAY_____ /_____ /_____